JUNE PETERS, YOU WILL CHANGE THE WORLD ONE DAY

WRITTEN BY **ALIKA TURNER**

ILLUSTRATED BY **NAAFI NR**

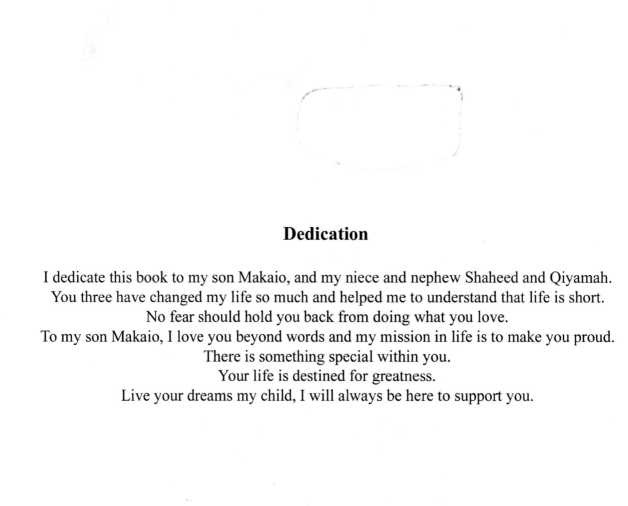

Dedication

I dedicate this book to my son Makaio, and my niece and nephew Shaheed and Qiyamah.
You three have changed my life so much and helped me to understand that life is short.
No fear should hold you back from doing what you love.
To my son Makaio, I love you beyond words and my mission in life is to make you proud.
There is something special within you.
Your life is destined for greatness.
Live your dreams my child, I will always be here to support you.

Ordering Information:

Quantity sales. Special discounts are available on quantity purchases by corporations, associations, and others. For details, contact the publisher at the address above.

Printed in the United States of America

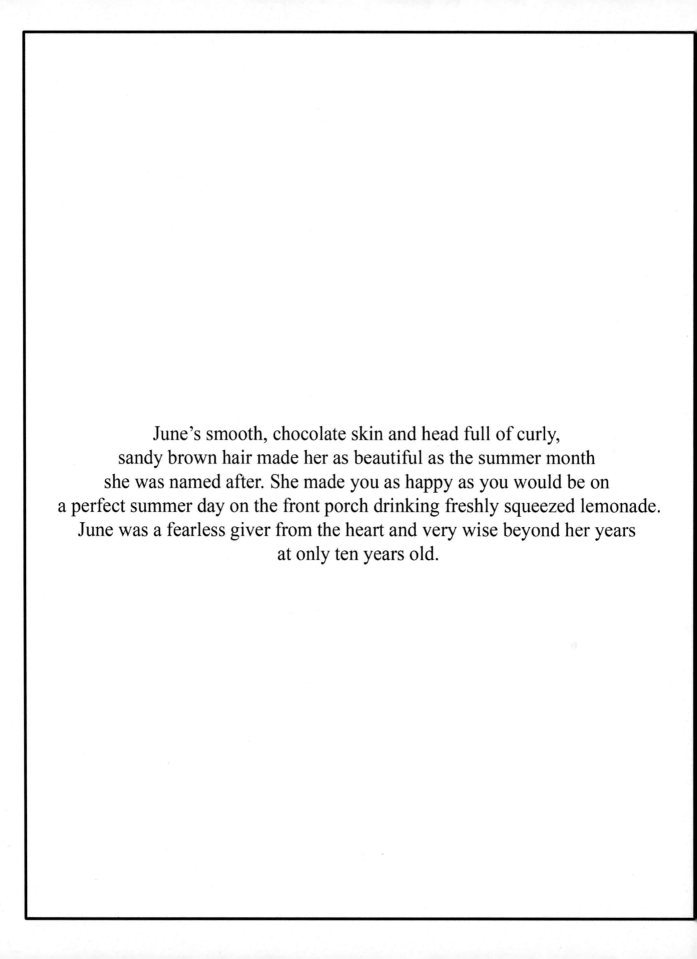

June's smooth, chocolate skin and head full of curly,
sandy brown hair made her as beautiful as the summer month
she was named after. She made you as happy as you would be on
a perfect summer day on the front porch drinking freshly squeezed lemonade.
June was a fearless giver from the heart and very wise beyond her years
at only ten years old.

June repeatedly begged her parents to let her walk to school
by herself on multiple occasions.

"I am in the 5th grade," she said. June had always been
a very good student. She received excellent grades
in school and never got in trouble.

"I am responsible," she said. June was much more responsible
than her older brothers. She did not have to be told
to clean her room or to do any of her chores around the house.

"I don't have far to walk, "she said. June made a strong case,
especially considering that her school was only
one block away from their home.

Finally, her parents agreed to give her a chance for one week.

On her way to school, June noticed a man on
the side of the street asking people for change. She reached into her pocket
and pulled out the three dollars her mom had given her for lunch.
Walking very slowly, she thought about what she could do to
help the man who seemed sad. June began thinking about what it may
have felt like to be hungry or homeless. She was upset at the thought.
She knew what she had to do. She approached the homeless man,

"Here you are, sir."

June placed all her lunch money in the hat that he was holding.

"Bless you, child. You have no idea the difference you are making. Thank you."

The homeless man was beyond grateful for June's kindness. He continued to say thank you, even as she walked away.

Although now June would have no money for lunch after giving away all of hers, she felt so good inside that she skipped the whole way to school, smiling from ear to ear.

Throughout her day at school, June told all of her friends about what she had done for the homeless man on the street and how it made her feel.

At the end of the school day, June's mom was outside
waiting to pick her up.

Still excited about that morning, June immediately
began telling her mom all about helping the homeless man
on her way to school.

Her mom simply smiled and explained to June
that she needed to be more aware of strangers and that giving away
her lunch money was not acceptable.

Her mom began talking in a very stern voice.
"June, I understand you want to help people and that is fine.
However, you need to be careful at all times. There are strangers everywhere.
Some are good and some are bad. Your dad and I decided to
let you walk to school because you proved to us that you were responsible."

June hung her head low. She was sad that
she had disappointed her mom.

"Mom, I'm sorry," she replied.
"I understand what you are saying,
but there are lots of people without food or a place to live
and I just want to help them. Sometimes when I'm at school,
I'm not hungry at lunch and I waste my food."

"June, baby, you have a heart of gold.
Maybe we can come up with another way to help.
Until then, young lady, no more talking with strangers.
Do you understand?"

"Yes, ma'am," June said reluctantly.

June did not really understand why her mom was so upset,
but she agreed that she would no longer give
lunch money away or talk with strangers.

The next morning, June walked to school with her older brother Jay.

"Why do you have to come with me, Jay? I'm a big girl," June said,
as she walked far in front of him.

"You are talking to strangers and giving your money away.
Mom doesn't like that," Jay shouted, trying to catch up with June.

Jay told his sister that sometimes strangers look nice and harmless.

He explained, "Some of those strangers are not so nice.
It's best that you don't talk to anyone on your way to school."
Jay went on to tell his sister that if it were important to her,
he would give the homeless man the few dollars he had.

"Really, Jay? You're the best," June responded.
Jay handed June four dollars from his pocket that
he had been saving for a day at the arcade.

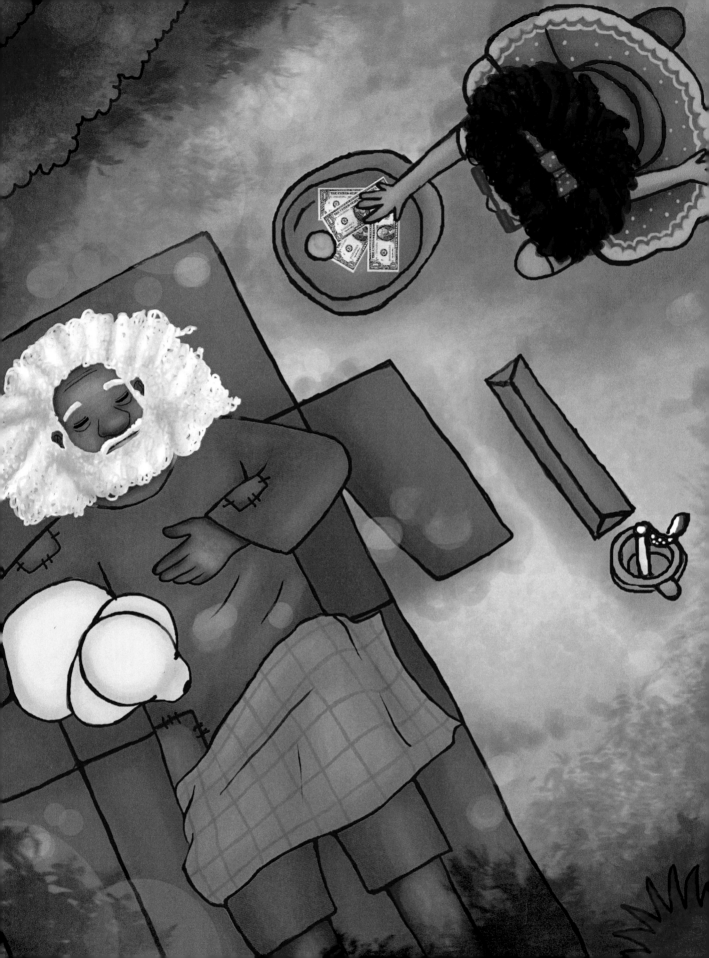

June noticed the homeless man from the other day.
He was sleeping. She did not want to wake him,
so she gently placed the dollars from her brother
into the man's hat. As she turned to walk away, she heard the man say,
"Thank you, young lady. You're remarkable and
you will change the world one day."

Those words stuck with June throughout the entire day.
She continued to hear the man's last words in her head:
"You will change the world one day."

Every night at dinnertime, for as long as June could remember, her family would take turns talking about the good things that had happened that day. June loved doing this. She always had something incredible to share and that evening, was no different.

"June-baby, it's your turn," her mom said.

She began by telling her parents that she was sorry for talking to strangers and giving her money away. She also shared with them that she had figured out a way that she could help people.

"Mom, Dad, I want to make lunches for the homeless and give them out."

"June, what you just shared with us is amazing.
Your dad and I would love to help.
We can make a whole day out of it and invite
the neighbors and your friends to join us,"
her mom proudly responded.

"Count us in June," Jay said.

June was elated by all the support she had received from her family.
After dinner, she grabbed her pen and notepad.
Sitting on the couch, she wrote down all of her ideas.
At the top of the page, June wrote:

JUNE'S FEED THE HOMELESS DAY

Her parents sat down on the couch and asked all about her plans
and how they could help make it a great success.

"Mom and Dad, I would like to do this in the park on Saturday.
We could give out sandwiches, bottled water, and fruit
to all the homeless people."
June told her parents what she wanted everyone in the family to do.
"Dad, will you make the flyers? Mom, will you get all of the
neighbors and our friends involved? I will ask my brothers to
help me fix the lunches."

"June-baby you have this all figured out. I'll get started," Dad said.

"So will I," her mom responded.

A few days before June's big event, she went with her brothers
around the neighborhood. They passed out flyers to everyone and
made sure to give each homeless person one too.

June noticed the man she had helped sitting at the bus stop.
"Hello sir. I would like to invite you to my event at the park this Saturday,"
she said as she handed him a flyer

The man looked over the flyer and immediately looked up, smiling at June.
"Young lady, I told you that you would change the world one day.
I will most certainly be there."

June smiled at the man and waved goodbye.

It was finally Saturday morning, the day of:
JUNE'S FEED THE HOMELESS DAY.

June and her brothers had been up all morning making lunches.
Her parents were steadily packing the car with everything they needed.
Rachel, June's best friend, showed up early to help along with the neighbors.

"Is everyone ready?" her dad enthusiastically asked in his loud voice.

"Yes, sir!" was the response from everyone there.

As June, her family, neighbors, and friends
pulled up to the park, they notice the long
line of homeless men and women already waiting.
"Wow! Dad, did you do that?"
June asked while looking at the
large banner that read:

JUNE'S
FEED THE HOMELESS DAY

"Yes, June-baby, I did,"

"Thank you, Dad, thank you. I love it."

All of June's family and friends
began passing out the lunches.
Everyone was pleased and very
impressed that such a young girl
could have a big heart.
June could not stop smiling.

"Hello young lady," a man said, standing next
in line for his lunch. June looked up
and noticed that it was the man she had been
giving her money to the last few mornings
before school.

"Hello sir, I was waiting for you.
I have a special lunch just for you."

June handed him a big bag from under the table.

The man looked inside and smiled at June. "Bless you."
"I told you that one day you would change the world."

The End

Acknowledgments

To Stephen, thank you for always being so supportive and listening when I talked day and night about this book.

I love you

About the Author

Alika was born in Richmond, California and currently resides in Lithonia, Georgia at the age of 32 she knew it was time to focus on her dream to become a children's book author. Her amazing son Makaio gave her so much inspiration during and after her writing process for this book.

When she started developing June's character, she thought a lot about the person she is now and the child she wanted to be. Alika enjoys writing amazing children's books, which targets children ages 5-12. These stories aim to encourage young children, to be amazing in life now and as they grow up to become mature adults.

There is no limit to what our children can do. It is our job as parents to support them and their dreams. You never know the blessing you can be to others until you have accepted the gift god has given you.
- Alika

About the Illustrator

Naafi is an illustrator from Indonesia. Since childhood she loved to draw. At the young age of 24, she realized her dream of becoming a professional illustrator. She loves the world of children's illustration, it holds a special place in her heart.

In her life, she stands by this principle *"Dreams will only be a dreams if we do nothing to make them become reality".* This book is a perfect example of making dreams a reality.

It is an honor for Naafi to illustrate this book and others in the June Peters series.

Do not forget, create the history of life as beautiful as possible.

JUNE'S FAMILY

WRITTEN BY **ALIKA TURNER**
ILLUSTRATED BY **NAAFI NR**

JASMINE (MOM)

JAY

JUNE

GIVING
IS
GOLDEN

CARL (DAD)

JEREMY

JUSTIN

Made in the USA
Middletown, DE
07 May 2017